FROGGY GREEN

Anna Walker

Kane/Miller
BOOK PUBLISHERS

Everyone likes

different colors.

Sam likes
fireman red.

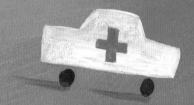

Olive likes
fairy pink.

Lucy likes
polka dot orange.

Milly likes
sunshine yellow.

Joe likes
froggy green.

Tess likes
sky blue.

Charlie likes
monster purple.

But everyone loves ...

rainbow ice cream!